*This Book is dedicated to my Parents,
and to my Russian Literature Teacher –
Elena Stepanovna Nikiforova.*

*It's been published in memory
of my husband, who inspired me
to publish my poetry.*

Copyright © 2024 by Margarita Furer

All rights reserved. No part of this publication may be reproduced, distributed or transmitted in any form or by any means, including photocopying, recording, or other electronic or mechanical methods, without the prior written permission of the publisher, except in the case of brief quotations embodied in critical reviews and certain other noncommercial uses permitted by copyright law. For permission requests, write to the publisher, addressed "Attention: Permissions Coordinator," at the address below.

Margarita Furer / Author's Tranquility Press
3900 N Commerce Dr. Suite 300 #1255
Atlanta, GA 30344
www.authorstranquilitypress.com

Ordering Information:
Quantity sales. Special discounts are available on quantity purchases by corporations, associations, and others. For details, contact the "Special Sales Department" at the address above.

For your Mind, For your Heart, For your Soul / Margarita Furer
Paperback: 978-1-964037-58-5
eBook: 978-1-964037-59-2

Why do I write Poetry?

It is a good question: "Why do I write?"
But there is no answer or hint.
It could be a way to express my mind,
The way I feel, and I think.
Maybe a page is my battle ring
To fight an anger and lie.
Maybe it is an Angel's wing,
Which makes me feel free and fly.
It is my sail in a life's stormy sea.
Expending Horizon's line
It is my dreaming time machine
Fueled by the Soul's rhyme.
It is a good question: "Why do I write?"
But there is no answer or hint.
My Pen-Ship is ready, the word- knots are tied.
Just wish me a fair Wind.

Kids' Corner

I CAN

Why do you think I cannot go?
I am already ONE.
I speak, I cry, I laugh, I grow,
And I can even run.

Why do you think I cannot count?
I am already TWO.
There are so many things around.
One, Two, and Three, and Ugh!!!

Chorus
Children, Children, you grow so fast.
Children, Children, life is your only test.
Nothing's coming without tears and pain.
But if you wish, you're only one who can.

Why do you think I cannot read?
I am already THREE.
I'm so happy when I meet
My dear "ABC".

Why do you think I can't design?
I am already FOUR.
The whole unknown world is mine,
But I'll discover more.

Chorus.
It is unfair - I cannot vote.
I am already FIVE.
Ask me of presidents. I know
And even "Bill Of Rights".

You will be SIX, and more, and then
You'll have success and win,
If don't lose these words "I CAN",
Because it's your engine.

Chorus

"WHY?" asking girl

My little girl - she wants to know
About everything around.
Her tiny "Why" is in every corner.
But it can grow into a giant.

Chorus
Who glued the clouds to the sky?
Why can't I fly like a butterfly?
Who shows us the funny and the scary dreams?
Is it at night a Honeymoon?
Will Honeysun be coming soon?
You say I am an angel, then where are my wings?
Who cut my wings?

How much it cost a heart of gold?
If I am beauty where is my beast?
Is Ford a car we can afford?
Dad, could you show your iron fist?

Chorus
"WHY?" asking girl, "WHY?" asking girl,
We cannot stand it anymore.
"WHY"'s everywhere, in everyone, in everything,
In our brains, on our tongs, in our dreams, in our songs.
Ooh, could you stop, give us a rest, and start to think?
Please, start to think.

But I'm afraid the rest of live
We'll solve "WHY?" asking girl's crosswords,
Because she grows up with her "WHY?"
By changing topics and the words.

Chorus
And life is like a riddle cake.
Each piece is cut with lots of try
By making billions of mistakes
To answer all these endless" WHY".
Who tells me why, please?

Free Translation from Russian
Lyrics Y.Entin, Music M. Minkov

The Road of Kindness

If you ask life to show what road you should go,
Because there are so many roads you can go through,
You should the Sun follow, although this way's unknown.
The Road of Kindness is the only faithful way for you.
You should the Sun follow, although this way's unknown.
The Road of Kindness is the only faithful way for you.

Forget about your worries, all fall and take-off stories,
And don't whine if obstacles hold you from dreams come true.
And if your friend's in trouble don't count on a wonder.
Hurry up to help. The Road of Kindness is one way for you.
And if your friend's in trouble don't count on a wonder.
Hurry up to help. The Road of Kindness is one way for you.

They're getting your attention – the doubts and temptations.
Remember – Life's a challenge, and it's not a children's play.
Say "no" to the flaws, follow major laws,
Which prove that Road of Kindness is the most faithful way.
Say "no" to the flaws, follow major laws,
Which prove that Road of Kindness is the most faithful way.

If you ask life to show what road you should go,
Because there are so many roads you can go through,
You should the Sun follow, although this way's unknown.
The Road of Kindness is the only faithful way for you.
You should the Sun follow, although this way's unknown.
The Road of Kindness is the only faithful way for you.
Free Translation from Russian

Lyrics Yuriy Entin, music V. Thomas

The Dance of the little Ducks

Everyone wants 'be like us –
Funny, clumsy, little Ducks,
Funny, clumsy, little Ducks
Pa-Pa-Pa-Pa
Even Hippo big and fat
Sings, and dances, plays clarinet,
Sings, and dances, plays clarinet,
Pa-Pa-Pa-Pa

Chorus
Let's bring back the Childhood
With its crazy Charm.
We are now Ducklings,
And Life is Wonder, And Life is Fun.

It is easy be like us,
Join, enjoy our dancing Class,
Join, enjoy our dancing Class.
Pa-Pa-Pa-Pa
Put the sadness on the shelf,
Be like Children, be yourself,
Be like Children, be yourself.
Pa-Pa-Pa-Pa

Chorus

Free Translation from Russian
Lyrics L. Oshanin, music E. Kolmanovskiy

I'm working as a Sorcerer

I am flying through the Sea and Land.
Who can tell me where I'll be tomorrow?
I bring water to the desert sand,
And a happiness instead of sorrow.

Chorus
Why? I'll tell you what a wise man says:
"It is life, which teaches you what is truly fair."
Simple, I am working as. Simple, I am working as.
Simple, I am working as a sorcerer, a sorcerer.

I can see you in the winter frost,
And your steps 'like dots in a white board corner.
Let me talk to you, and be your host,
Making way much shorter and much warmer.

Chorus
A new star sparks in the skies like pearl,
And the maple trees sing acapella.
If you think you are not pretty girl,
I'll convince 'you look like Cinderella.

Chorus
Helping others is my major rule,
And of cause is caring, sharing, smiling.
It's my only secret, and my tool.
You can trust me it is worth of trying.

Chorus
Why? I'll tell you what a wise man says:
"Let the life to teach you what is truly fair."
Then you'll be able working as, you'll be able working as,
You'll be able working as a sorcerer, a sorcerer.

Fee Translation from Russian
Samuil Marshak

Tired Mom came home from her Work.
She opened the door and ooh…
Exhausted with what she found,
She looked scared to death around…
"Was the house under attack?"
"No."
"Was it crossed by a truck?"
"No.'
"Was here a hurricane?"
"No."
"Was it a crash of a plane?"
"No."
"It might be not our floor."
"Our."
"Did I open not our door?"
"Our."
"Does it mean it was an earthquake?"
"No, mommy, give me a break.
It was just my old friend Pete.
We played here a little bit."

Free Translation from Russian
Lyrics A. Timofeevskiy, music V. Shainskiy

Crocodile Gena's Song
From the cartoon "Cheburashka"

Let pedestrians clumsily jump and run through the puddles,
Let the street look like 'river today.
It's unclear to the people why I'm so funny
On this rainy and cloudy day.

Chorus
And I am playing my Accordion,
Want my happiness to share.
So sorry, that my birthday
Comes just once a year.

All of sudden a wizard lands in 'blue helicopter,
Shows movies for free on 'big screen.
He will say, "Happy Birthday!"
Maybe will give as 'present
Hundred servings delicious ice cream.

Chorus

Lyrics

* * *

In any time, for any ages
I'm sure Love is the major thing-
Life's deepest meaning, its happiest pages.
If people love, it means they live.

* * *

You are with me, and 'night seems so short.
You are with me – my dream, my life, my Lord.
You're my moonlight, my sunrise, my sunset.
You are my North, my South, East, and West.

You're heaven's gift, my future, present, past,
My only Love, which I believe will last.
You're everything what Man can only be.
May God bless you, and let you be with me.

* * *

Without you my life is just a word.
You worry me – my mind, my heart, my soul.
You can't replace to me the whole World,
But it looks like you do or maybe know.

Like everyone I have my own things –
My kids, and friends, good and bad luck, success,
But I need you – the One who gave me wings,
Who let me understand 'true happiness.

Free Translation from Russian
Lyrics L. Utyosov

They're so many girls around
Whom to avoid is pretty tough.
But only one makes your song sound
Like you're in heaven not on Ground
When you're in love.

Love comes to you without warning,
And gives your life a rocket swing,
Turns everything what's sad and boring
Into exciting and rewarding,
And makes you sing:

Chorus
My heart, thanks for refusing quiet season,
Thank you for making me dream and believe.
My heart, I know that she is a reason
That you have chosen my Love as only way to live.

There is a magic power we own

There is a magic power we own –
Easy to lose and difficult to find.
It's like a song familiar but unknown,
So wild and tough, but also tender, kind.

Chorus
If you want you can have it,
If you're wise you will keep it.
It's a light, it's a treasure
We can feel but cannot measure.

There is a magic power we own
For which we live and die, we cry and laugh.
It's peoples' dream, it is a feeling's crown
With 'simple, valuable name of LOVE.

Chorus

Free Translation from Russian
Lyrics N. Dobronravov, S. Grebennikov, music A. Pachmutova

Tenderness

Earth' a deserted place without you,
Only hours are left to live,
But as always leaves fall in the woods,
And a crowd of cars rushes through the streets.
But it's so empty, I'm alone.
You are in the sky
And you fly, and the stars
Give you as 'present - their tenderness.

It was also empty in the world
At that time when flew Exupery,
As today the leaves fell in the fall,
And the Earth couldn't imagine it
How to live without him until
He came back from sky,
But he flew, and the stars
Gave him as 'present - their tenderness.

Earth' a deserted place without you,
If you can then fly to me, I'll wait...

Greeting on Valentine's Day
For Him

You make me laugh when I'm sad and crying,
You make me cry from fun with happy tears,
You make me feel having the wings and flying
As I'm your princess, and you are my prince.
A fairy tale, a Cinderella story
Happened to me today, in real life.
I'm grateful for a wonder and a glory
Of having you, my dear in my life.

For Her

You make me laugh when I'm feeling down,
You make me cry from fun with happy tears,
You make me feel wearing the royal crown
As you're my princess and I am your prince.
A fairy tale became a real story
Of you and me, and our endless Love.
I'm grateful for a wonder and a glory
Of having you, my dear in my life.

Greeting for my daughter's wedding

Do you remember a moment when you met -
Two strangers, exchanging "Hi "?
But it was a spark, the warm waves' been sent
When you looked in each other's eyes.

You went through a lot both good and bad,
But it just strengthened the ties.
You know – beside you is your best friend,
When you look in each other's eyes.

The Life is not only the fun and bloom.
It has its "Low" s and "High" s,
But you can have life lasting Honeymoon
If you look in your loved one's eyes.

I wish when you marry one day your kids,
Sharing secrets of the family lives,
You could say: "The main rule of the Happiness is -
Look more often in your Loved One's Eyes."

Greeting for my son's wedding

You are talented. You are strong and kind,
You are 'beautiful source of warmth and light.
It's a miracle – meeting 'soulmate.
You have used your chance,
It's time to celebrate.

And I want to wish Bride and Groom today
"Stay in love 'whole life as at your wedding day.
You have found your one - most precious gift.
Cherish whom you have. Mazel Tov, my kids.

My little Prince

Who has imagined you?
It's a wonderland.
I keep this sparkling view
Through the timeless sand.
Your image's in my dreams
Real or not it seems.
Where is the way to you, my little Prince?

No matter deep or high
Far or very close
Light of your smiling eyes,
And your tender voice
Will bring me to your world
To tell you just three words
Known by only Two
That I love you.

Who has imagined you?
It's a wonderland.
I keep this sparkling view
Through the timeless sand.
Your image's in my dreams
Real or not it seems.
I'll find my way to you, my little Prince
From my dreams.

For your Mind

For your Heart

For your Soul

Immigrants

We are different people from different countries.
We speak different languages and have different cultures.
But it doesn't matter where we are from,
Here is now our home.
And life can be better than ever had been
If it doesn't matter the color of skin,
If it doesn't matter where we are from,
And what is there society form.
Yes, we are different, but alike to each other,
Like very close friends, like sisters and brothers.
Let us not decide who is better or worse,
Because all of us are the children of Earth.

Kindness

It is very hard to be a kind human.
No matter if you are a man or a woman.
Kindness is a talent of soul, its care.
We need it like water, or food, or air.

It's not a weakness, with a kind word
We can fight an anger in our world.
Do not be afraid of being kind
Not just in your dreams – in your life, in your mind.

* * *

I want to be a bluebird flying in the sky,
I want to be a flower that's beautiful and shy,
I want to be a treasure, a knowledge full bookshelf,
But wishing to be something I want to stay myself.

Spring

Do you know what I think about?
Do you know what is on my mind?
Stop for a moment, listen, look around.
Do you see how peaceful it's, how bright?
Do you see the Nature born from nothing,
Rainbow of flowers, birds' chorus, life full rain?
What are sicknesses, or troubles – all the bad things,
If I feel each spring – I'm born again?

* * *

White and black,
Forward, back.
Wide, and tight.
Wrong and right.

But we live in the multicolor world.
It can't be described with the opposite words.
A person cannot be just bad or good.
And what about your health and mood?

Do not look at people and their lives
Just up and down, from the left or the right.
You can be the happiest person around,
If you can see Sun in the sky not just a ground.

My Verrazano Bridge

And there it stands so powerful but light
Spreading its wings from' n island to the island.
A cloud is hugging its steel torso tight,
Resting its head on a stone chest of a giant.

Its eagle eyes are guarding see and land
High from the sky – man's crafted constellation.
You're Staten Island's lifeway, helping hand,
Its pride and beauty beyond imagination.

My Angel, my white Knight

(the story of a little white puppy that saved my life)
Her days and nights were mixed in a furious bowl
With a tremendous pain, and hell like fever.
Her body weakened, but her warrior's soul
Was screaming: "Dying should be my decision."

It was a morning full of warmth and light.
But it was there – in another world.
And there he came – her angel, her White Knight.
No matter that he didn't have a sword.

His ringing voice, his energy, his style
To move (he didn't walk, he ran).
And played with her a little bit, a while,
And something happened – a miracle began.

Life-giving waves from his dark sparkling eyes
Woke up her hidden strength, brought back belief.
He was so funny, playful, friendly, nice,
That broke the illness, bringing a relief.

That very day she gave herself an oath
To help those who're in need, not let them fail.
No need to be a wizard or a ghost
To make somebody's life a fairytale.

Free Translation from Russian
Lyrics V.Korostyilev, V.Lifshits, Music A.Lepin

The song about a good mood

If you feel unlucky, nothing makes you happy,
Doesn't make you funny even sunny day,
'Smile of any stranger can be very helpful.
It will make you smiling anywhere, anyway.

Chorus
Smiles of people as the magicians
Light the fire in your eyes.
And a good mood, the friendly wishes
Will stay with you, with all of us.

If you're disappointed with your friend's behavior,
If he can betray you even in hard time,
You will meet another, much more valuable,
Who'll become a real friend and will bring back your smile.

Chorus
If you had a quarrel with the lovely woman,
What without reason people do in rush,
Look just at each other with a smile and humor.
Sometimes better than the words Smile can speak for us.

Chorus

Free Translation from Russian
Lyrics R. Rozhdestvenskiy, Music G. Movsesyan

My Years- my Treasure

No matter that my hair is gray,
I'm not afraid of winter's weather.
Not only sadness built my way,
They are my Years – my wealth, my treasure.
No matter that my hair is gray,
Not only sadness built my way,
They are my Years – my wealth, my treasure.

I pushed my time not to be late,
Worked for the people, and for pleasure,
And don't regret no money saved.
I have my Years – my wealth, my treasure.
I pushed my time not to be late,
And don't regret no money saved.
I have my Years – my wealth, my treasure.

So let them say: "it's close my end".
Light of my star cannot be measured,
And I believe that baby's hand
One day will raise my Years – my treasure.
So let them say: "it's close my end".
But I believe that baby's hand
One day will raise my Years – my treasure.

Free interpretation from Russian
Lyrics M. Dyarfash, Music G. Gladkov

Wake up and sing!

Our world is full of magic,
Mixture of funny things and tragic,
But it becomes more colorful with songs.
They're our friends, and our courage,
Our treasure, and a storage
Of everything around what's right and wrong.

Chorus
Wake up and sing, wake up and sing.
Let's free your spirit and sense.
Who knows if your life will give another chance?
Don't forget that success
Chooses who take their chance,
Laugh at themselves more than at anybody else.
Sing when you dream,
Sing waking up.
Songs are your wealth.

If you're on top, and you are winning,
You can be happier with singing.
Let Lady Luck to smile to you all the way.
But if you feel the hell around,
Lonely fight with underground.
Song is your sword to fight bad luck away.

Chorus

Who is a real Friend?

Who is a real Friend
How to understand?
(To measure the height and weight
And later to calculate,
Or to invent some unit
Or some Device – a friend chip?
You don't have to do it
To determine a friendship.
But there is a measurement
Of those relationship –
Your Friend's soft, but helpful hand
Given to you when you need it.

Each age has its own unbeatable beauty.

Each Age has its own unbeatable beauty.
A baby is born to discover this world,
To bring to it its angelic purity,
To answer all, Why? Who? When? Where? And What?

The toddlers start measuring feet, yards, and miles
On their journey through the Unknown.
The Smiles on the faces, the sparks in the eyes
Are signs – the enjoyment of life has been grown.

The years through school with the so many first:
First Teacher, first grade, first friend, and first love.
An ocean of feelings, a knowledge thirst –
They are as beautiful as they are tough.

You feel like an architect, building your world,
Creating a castle from the mess.
And no obstacles, no words
Can stop you on your way to success.

It's time when you hold your baby tight –
Your little angel, your precious treasure.
And no restless days, and no sleepless nights
Can ruin your endless parenting pleasure.

The time's starting flying with the speed of light –
Your 30th, your 40th, your 50th spot.
The knowledge, experience are on your side.
Who cares – you're called grand,
If you are still hot.

Your 60th – is your retirement station,
A not easy task to push your life's breaks.
But this is a time to teach a new generation,
To build a strong bond that relationship makes.

Your 70th, 80th. It's close a final check,
But you are grateful for each day's been rendered.
The love and the time that you shared are paid back.
If you're not around, you'll still be remembered.

Each Age has its own unbeatable beauty,
Like writing a poem about lifetime,
And if you can learn having fun in the duties,
You'll find for your age a suitable rhyme.

www.ingramcontent.com/pod-product-compliance
Lightning Source LLC
LaVergne TN
LVHW040203080526
838202LV00042B/3297